THE SWEETEST VALENTINE

BuzzPop

BuzzPop

An imprint of Bonnier Publishing USA
251 Park Avenue South, New York, NY 10010
All rights reserved, including the right of
reproduction in whole or in part in any form.
BuzzPop is a trademark of Bonnier Publishing
USA, and associated colophon is a trademark of
Bonnier Publishing USA.
Manufactured in China HOX 0918
First Edition 1 3 5 7 9 10 8 6 4 2
ISBN 978-1-4998-0784-4
buzzpopbooks.com
bonnierpublishingusa.com

Under license by:
©2018 Moose Enterprise (INT) Pty Ltd. Shoppies™
logos, names, and characters are licensed
trademarks of Moose Enterprise (INT) Pty Ltd.
29 Grange Road, Cheltenham, VIC 3192, Australia
www.moosetoys.com
info@moosetoys.com

On the day before Valentine's Day, Strawberry Kiss was excited to make Valentine's Day cards for her friends. First she drew some pretty flowers on a card for Cheeky Chocolate. Then she made a large heart for Kooky Cookie's card and lots of tiny hearts for Miss Pressy's.

"And now for the hard part!" she said to herself. She thought very carefully, and then in her best handwriting, she wrote a poem for each of her friends telling them why they're so special. She started with Cheeky Chocolate.

I love the way you are,
you're always so very sweet.
I think you are a star,
to be with you is a treat.
HAPPY VALENTINE'S DAY!

Then she wrote a poem for Kooky Cookie.

You help me every day,
you're so kind and true.
I'm so very lucky
to have a friend like you.
HAPPY VALENTINE'S DAY!

And finally she crafted one just for Miss Pressy.

You always know just what to say,
your smile is like the sun.
You brighten up every day
for me and everyone!
HAPPY VALENTINE'S DAY!

Cheeky Chocolate

Kooky Cookie

Miss Pressy

Happy with her cards, Strawberry Kiss placed them carefully in their envelopes and placed them on a shelf in the Small Mart before heading home for the night.

I can't wait to see my friends' faces when they read their cards! she thought happily.

Strawberry Kiss woke up early on Valentine's Day. She ran straight to the Small Mart, eager to give out her cards.

But when she went back to the shelf, her Valentine's cards weren't there!

Apple Blossom walked into the aisle and Strawberry Kiss told her about the missing cards.

"They must have fallen off the shelf," Apple Blossom said. "But I bet they're nearby!" They searched up and down the aisle, but they couldn't find Strawberry Kiss's cards anywhere!

Strawberry Kiss decided to search Shopville for the cards. First she visited the boutique, but no one had seen the cards. Then she went to the bakery, but she had no luck there either.

Just as she stepped into the ice cream shop, Apple Blossom called to her, "Strawberry Kiss, I forgot to wish you a happy Valentine's Day!"

"Oh!" said Strawberry Kiss. "Happy Valentine's Day to you, too!"

And these cheery words gave Strawberry Kiss an idea.

"I shouldn't waste Valentine's Day looking for the cards," she told herself. "I'll have to do something else to show my friends how much they mean to me." She bought an ice cream cone to help her think.

"I know!" she cried. "I will do sweet things for my sweet friends!" She headed straight for the Small Mart, waving to other Shopkins along the way.

First she found Cheeky Chocolate.

"Happy Valentine's Day!" she called out.

But Cheeky Chocolate was too busy trying to pick up a bunch of cans from the floor. "I slipped and knocked over the pile of cans on the shelf," she said with a sigh.

"Don't worry! I'll help you clean up," replied Strawberry Kiss cheerfully. "It will be my Valentine's Day present to you!" In no time, the two friends had placed all the cans back on the shelf.

"You're such a good friend!" said Cheeky Chocolate gratefully.

Feeling much happier, Strawberry Kiss stepped outside the Small Mart and smiled when she saw the pretty flowers at the shop. *These will be just right for Miss Pressy*, she thought as she picked a beautiful bouquet.

She walked along with the flowers until she found Miss Pressy outside the burger bar.

"Happy Valentine's Day!" cried Strawberry Kiss as she handed Miss Pressy the bouquet. "These are for being such a good friend."

"That's the kindest present anyone's given me all year!" said Miss Pressy with a smile.

Strawberry Kiss didn't have far to go before she bumped into Kooky Cookie, who was struggling to carry dozens of Valentine's Day decorations.

"Happy Valentine's Day!" said Strawberry Kiss. "I'll help you carry those."

Strawberry Kiss even volunteered to help Kooky Cookie decorate the Small Mall for the Valentine's Day party.

She had so much fun helping her friend that she forgot all about the missing Valentine's Day cards.

When all the decorations were hung, Strawberry Kiss volunteered to get snacks for the party.

On her way out of the Small Mart, she ran into Apple Blossom. She was holding Valentine's cards that looked just like the ones Strawberry Kiss had made for her friends!

Kooky

Miss Pressy

"You said you were doing nice things for your friends, so I did something nice for you!" said Apple Blossom. "I searched the whole Small Mart and finally found your cards in another aisle. Happy Valentine's Day!"

"Thank you, Apple Blossom!" said Strawberry Kiss. "This is the best Valentine's Day gift you could have given me!"

Strawberry Kiss and Apple Blossom raced back to deliver the cards.

Strawberry Kiss and Apple Blossom found their friends gathering for the Valentine's Day party.

"These cards are for you!" Strawberry Kiss cried as she handed each of her friends an envelope. "They are from me and my special helper, Apple Blossom."

"It's beautiful!" said Cheeky Chocolate.

"This is perfect! Thank you," said Kooky Cookie.

"I love it!" said Miss Pressy.

Miss Pressy

Cheeky Choco

Kooky Cookie

"You know, Strawberry Kiss, this card means a lot to me," said Kooky Cookie. "But the way you helped me today means even more."

"And Apple Blossom's help meant a lot, too!" added Cheeky Chocolate.

"You're right," said Strawberry Kiss. "Friendship is the sweetest Valentine."